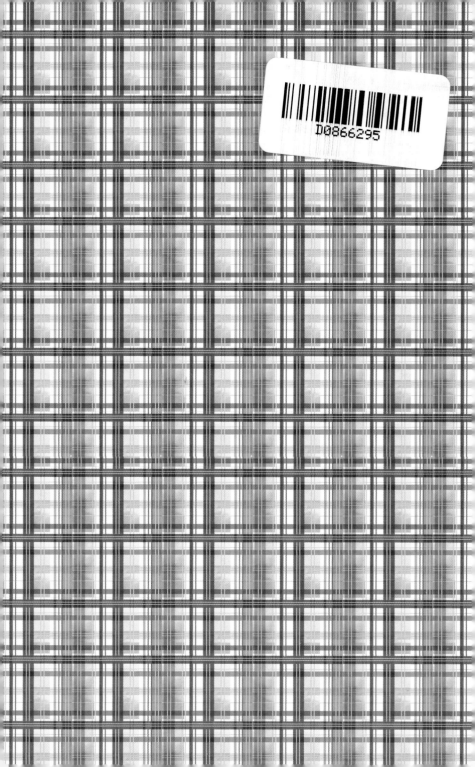

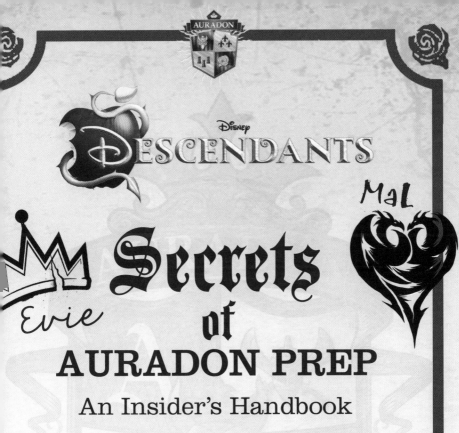

AURADON

Disney

DESCENDANTS

Mal

Evie

Secrets of AURADON PREP

An Insider's Handbook

JAY

CARLOS

Adapted by Matthew Sinclair Foreman

studio fun
INTERNATIONAL

TABLE OF CONTENTS

Bet I get a two-page spread!
—Audrey

Peeked— just one.
—Jay

Criminals!
—Audrey

Check this out!

ick!

Hey! Can the new guys even read?????

oviously!

AKA Loser Parade!

—Mal

o way! Spoiler alert! —Carlos

Can't we skip right to this part? -Evie

3

 # Welcome Students

As royal patrons of Auradon Prep, we would like to welcome you to an exciting new year. Here you will join other students and celebrate our proud tradition of excellence.

While we may have some unusual new faces, we assure everyone that this will be like any other year at Auradon Prep, where virtue and self-improvement will be encouraged by all.

We hope you will use this book for guidance through the coming terms, and also record your adventures, as you seek to fulfill your brightest potential.

King Beast and Queen Belle

Long Live Evil!

I'd like to offer a special welcome to our new students, especially those who have traveled a long way to be here. Though these shores may seem very different from the ones you come from, we want you to feel at home. I am sure that our classmates will be inviting and open-minded, and that whatever stories may complicate our past, our future is a hopeful one.

—Prince Ben

He would be cute if he was not such a royal ☐ -M

BEN

This is a big year for me, one I have dreamed of (and worried about) since I was a kid. Next month, I will be crowned King of Auradon. Hard for me to believe, too! It's a huge responsibility, and I want to thank everyone at school who has helped me on my way. I hope I can be the leader they deserve. In the meantime (and always, I hope), I'll be just regular old Ben. Let's keep working together to make this a place everyone can enjoy. See you around school!

DUDE

I scavenged food from local farms for a long time before stumbling onto the dumpster behind the school cafeteria. I've been at Auradon Prep ever since! When the students adopted me as their unofficial mascot, I started studying, too. Now I can roll over and shake a paw. To the newcomers: I know what it's like to live rough. All you need is love!

JANE

My mother might be a fairy—the Fairy Godmother, actually—but you'll find me really down to earth. I actually don't use magic at all, though at times I sure wish I could. I also don't have quite the royal blood as some of my classmates, but I work hard in class and would like to believe we're all equal as long as we try. I'm looking forward to learning from our exciting new students.

DOUG

I might be Dopey's son, but don't think I approach school that way—I'm in pretty much every club at Auradon Prep! I'm the bandleader, which is probably my favorite activity outside of (if you can believe it)...Chemistry! Yup, like my miner father, I'm fascinated by the materials that make up the natural world. I can't wait to meet some new faces in the lab, and if you see me in the hall, please say hi...ho!

Who's Who at Auradon Prep

AUDREY

People say I look a lot like my mother. You might have heard of her—Sleeping Beauty, one of the most beautiful women ever? It's only natural, I guess, that I'm dating Ben, who will be king next month. What will that make me? Seriously, I've got my own things going on, like coming up with new cheers. I am the head cheerleader. And did I mention I'm Ben's girlfriend? Oh, for our new students, everyone knows that, just like my mother, I like my beauty sleep, so if I'm not exactly nice to you before noon, it's just the way I am. Have a spiffy day!

CHAD

I might not be getting crowned next month, but I'm already a Prince Charming, just like my father! My family ruled for so long, I don't mind giving others a chance to shine. Because my mother, Cinderella, rose from poverty, I understand how important it is to give back. So if you want to be my friend, you'll need to step up and contribute. Don't worry, it'll make you feel like a better person. Just like me.

LONNIE

My mom, Mulan, taught me to seek my own true self. So I really like trying new things, because they teach me about who I am. My experiences have made me realize how lucky we are to go to such an awesome school. Not everyone does. A big thanks to our guest students for bringing their unique gifts—I'm sure we'll all learn lots from each other.

Number of good deeds done last year: **2056** (an all-time record!)

Number of royal students: **15**

Number of buildings: **22** (not including dungeon)

Teacher to student to fairy ratio: **9:2:1**

Number of years since last dragon attack: **62**

Size of campus: **18 acres** (including moat)

Height of tallest tower: **183 feet** (off limits, unless waking a princess from a curse)

Facts & Figures

Noted Achievements

 Last year's debate team won against the Falcons, for the question, "Should we grant more freedom to the inhabitants of the Isle of the Lost?"

 Tourney champs last 3 of 5 years. (Go, Knights!)

Famous Guest Speakers Last Year

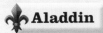 Aladdin

"Making Your Wishes Come True"

Ariel

"How to Stand on Your Own Two Feet— Even if You Used to Have a Tail!"

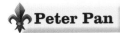 Peter Pan

"Growing Up Without Losing Your Inner Child"

History of Auradon

Once upon a time, Auradon was a land of mystery and wonder, where magic was rare but very powerful. Heroes and villains struggled against one another at every turn, and the tales of their adventures—Snow White hiding from the Evil Queen, the Dalmatians fleeing from Cruella de Vil, the saga of Maleficent and Sleeping Beauty—have been retold for generations.

King Beast, who ruled his corner of the map, saw everywhere the dangers that magic brought to the people. Truly, it was something he understood very personally. Selfish in his youth, King Beast had been cursed to live as an ugly monster until he found true love and broke the spell. It became his dream to create a new country where noble kindness was the greatest power of all.

12

Beast married the lovely Queen Belle and unified these many lands of legend into the United States of Auradon. Together with the powerful Fairy Godmother, his ally, he captured the villains that had long troubled all and imprisoned them on the Isle of the Lost.

With magic set aside—except for the rarest occasions— a modern era of peace and prosperity came to pass. Auradon and its people flourished, while the villains adapted to their new existence, starting businesses and families on the island. Most accepted their punishment. Yet we can never be certain.

Villainy, like magic, never goes away forever.

History of Auradon Prep

The formation of the United States of Auradon required a brand-new academy to shape the next generation of heroes. An old castle and its surrounding grounds were selected and converted into a preparatory school, and plans were made to welcome the first class. But a vital element was still lacking: a first principal for Auradon Prep.

After she created the magical barrier that contained the Isle of the Lost, Fairy Godmother put down her magic wand. Believing that the future lay in the new generation's hard work and careful study, she offered to lead the staff and students of Auradon Prep. Overjoyed, King Beast and Queen Belle accepted. And so the first term began.

Principal Profile

Of all the good fairies, Fairy Godmother is the most powerful. Since times of legend, she has done everything within her control to correct injustice in the world. When asked by King Beast to overcome the villains of Auradon, she knew it was a difficult but necessary step toward peace for all.

In her role as principal of Auradon Prep, Fairy Godmother encourages the personal and academic growth of the young people of Auradon with great lessons that come from ancient wisdom. Dedication to what may seem small often leads to significant results. While magic is powerful, hard work is more so. And even when people make mistakes, they always have the power to choose kindness and compassion.

These big responsibilities leave little time for entertainment, but Fairy Godmother believes that fun is important, too. If you're lucky, you can hear her perform with the Bibbidi-Bop all-woman barbershop quartet.

A continent built by magic, Auradon is home to a thriving modern society. Here, the latest art, science, and technology live alongside the heroism of an earlier age. Explore this rich landscape—from the natural wonders of Sherwood Forest and Desolation Point to the dramatic excitement of Neverland and Mount Olympus. There's adventure around every corner!

The epic towers of Auradon City rise from the cliffs above Belle's Harbor. Beyond, the growing centers of Charmington and Notre Dame gleam in the summer sun. On the other side of the river is the ritzy glamour of Camelot Heights, financial capital of the country.

Across the water from Cinderellasberg, through the polluted fog, lies the outline of the Isle of the Lost. Famous community of misfits and villains, the island is protected by a powerful force field that prevents anyone from going in or out—without permission of King Beast and Queen Belle.

Yeah, and villainy, too! Ha! —Mal

THE UNITED STATES OF AURADON

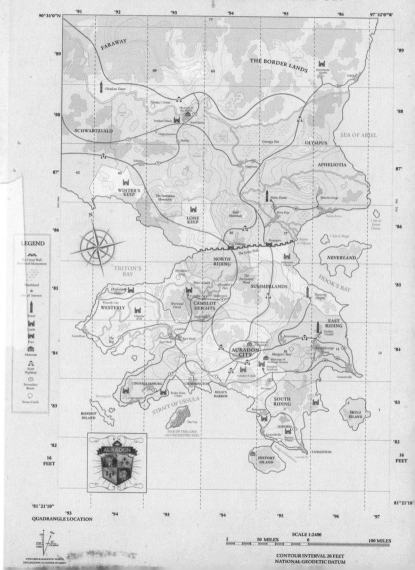

FARAWAY

THE BORDER LANDS

SCHWARTZVALD

WINTER'S KEEP

LONE KEEP

OLYMPUS

APHELIOTIA

SEA OF ARIEL

TRITON'S BAY

NORTH RIDING

SUMMERLANDS

NEVERLAND

HOOK'S BAY

WESTERLY

CAMELOT HEIGHTS

EAST RIDING

AURADON CITY

CINDERELLASBURG

CHARMINGTON

BELLE'S HARBOR

SOUTH RIDING

SKULL ISLAND

BONIFAY ISLAND

STRAIT OF URSULA

ISLE OF THE LOST
(ACCESS RESTRICTED)

AURORIA

TANGLETON

HISTORY ISLAND

LEGEND

The Great Wall
Historical Monument

Marshland

Site of Interest

Tower

Castle

Museum

State Highway

Secondary Route

Ferris Circle

AURADON

QUADRANGLE LOCATION

SCALE 1:2400

50 MILES   0   100 MILES

CONTOUR INTERVAL 20 FEET
NATIONAL GEODETIC DATUM

16 FEET

Don't worry, friends. When
we're done, all this will be ours!
Metaphorically speaking,
of course. —Mal

Ooh, Camelot Heights. I hear they
have the best boutiques there. -Evie

Forget it. We couldn't afford to
drink water in that town. —Mal

Wow. Home looks pretty small
from here. —Jay

And dirty. And fashion backward.
It's like the Dark Ages. -Evie

Couldn't they at least install wifi? —Carlos

Do you even know what that is? —Mal

Sure, it's—let me ask someone. —Carlos

17

Artifacts of the Realm

Those points look scary sharp. —Carlos

King Triton's Trident

I could sew a padded cover! —Evie

Origin: Inherited by King Triton from his father, Poseidon.

Powers Include: Firing bolts of magical energy, creating storms, transforming mermaids into humans.

Additional Information: Trident's powers may change according to the desire of the person using it.

Last Known Location: On display at the Museum of Cultural History.

Hey guys, this isn't interesting at all, hu —Mal

Spinning Wheel

Origin: Once ordinary, it was enchanted by Maleficent.

Nope! —Evie

Powers Include: May cause death and/or unending sleep.

Not at all. —Carlos

Additional Information: Prior to enchantment, once used to weave the king's underpants.

Last Known Location: On display at the Museum of Cultural History.

Triple n —Jay

The Glass Slipper

Those do not look comfortable. —Mal

Origin: Fairy Godmother's magic.
Powers Include: Shaped so perfectly by Fairy Godmother, it fits Cinderella alone.
Additional Information: Excellent for dancing.
Last Known Location: On display at the Museum of Cultural History.

Actually, they're a dream! —Audrey

Liar. They're a one-way ticket to Bunion City! —Carlos

Fairy Godmother's Wand

Origin: Summoned by Fairy Godmother.
Powers Include: Metamorphosis and enchantment, and can even manipulate time.
Additional Information: Said to have additional powers when combined with other magical artifacts. This hypothesis remains untested.
Last Known Location: On display at the Museum of Cultural History.

Artifacts of the Realm

Maleficent's Staff

Origin: Created magically from a broken tree branch.
Powers Include: Cursing, firing lightning bolts, summoning thorns.
Additional Information: Also known as "The Dragon's Eye."
Last Known Location: Isle of the Lost (its magic is disabled by our shield, so don't worry!).

Looks great for playing fetch with Dude. —Carlos

You crazy? He'd get fried! —Mal

Jafar's Snake Staff

Origin: Created by Jafar using a trapped spirit.
Powers Include: Hypnosis, telekinesis, and conjuration.
Additional Information: Its hypnotic powers are very strong, but not unbreakable.
Last Known Location: Destroyed by Aladdin, but suspected to have been rebuilt.

We could hypnotize teachers into giving us 100% on our finals! —Jay

Take it from me— cheating ain't all that. —Evie

Magic Mirror

Origin: Debated, but first known user was the Evil Queen.
Powers Include: Will reveal any knowledge to its owner.
Additional Information: Cannot predict future—so don't ask about tomorrow's lottery—but it's great for finding lost keys and phones.
Last Known Location: Presumed broken.

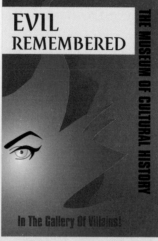

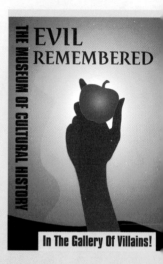

EVIL REMEMBERED

THE MUSEUM OF CULTURAL HISTORY

In The Gallery Of Villains!

EVIL REMEMBERED

THE MUSEUM OF CULTURAL HISTORY

In The Gallery Of Villains!

Explore Auradon's diverse and fascinating past! Here, history comes to life (except in cases where that would be far too dangerous). Curated by Queen Belle, the collection of artifacts reveals Auradon at its most magical, villainous, and heroic. Current programming includes:

Gallery of Heroes

From all walks of life, heroes and heroines rise to save the day. Sometimes they're princes and princesses whose fates command it, but at other times they are totally ordinary people inspired to greatness. And on rare occasions, someone who believes they are a villain discovers that under the surface, a hero is hiding. Come explore the exhibit and see if your inner hero emerges. We are not responsible for any daring acts that result!

Evil Remembered

Experience the thrill of confronting Auradon's most famous villains in the flesh, or at least as life-size statues. Standing face to face with these vicious scoundrels, you'll wonder if you could find the courage to stop their evil doings. Or does part of you envy their power? Custom dioramas show what horrors would come if ever they were set free. Don't worry—the real wrongdoers are trapped behind the Isle of the Lost's protective dome, so this display is 100% safe.

Maleficent

Jafar

Evil Queen

Cruella de Vil

Museum of Cultural History Map

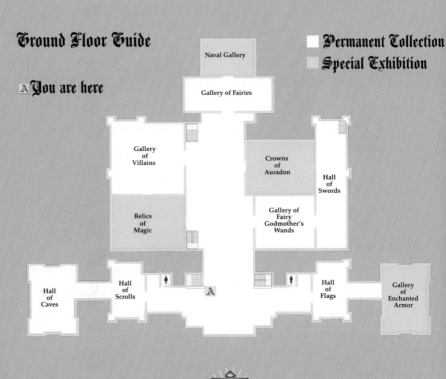

Ground Floor Guide

■ **Permanent Collection**

■ **Special Exhibition**

A **You are here**

Naval Gallery

Gallery of Fairies

Gallery of Villains

Crowns of Auradon

Hall of Swords

Relics of Magic

Gallery of Fairy Godmother's Wands

Hall of Caves

Hall of Scrolls

A

Hall of Flags

Gallery of Enchanted Armor

Exhibit Signs

Hall
of
Swords

Gallery
of
Fairies

Crowns
of
Auradon

Relics
of
Magic

Gallery of
Kings and
Queens

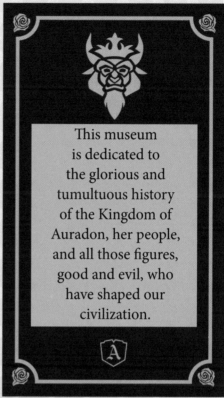

This museum is dedicated to the glorious and tumultuous history of the Kingdom of Auradon, her people, and all those figures, good and evil, who have shaped our civilization.

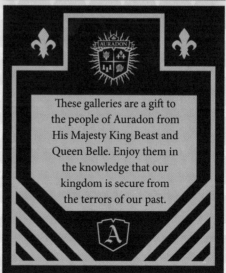

These galleries are a gift to the people of Auradon from His Majesty King Beast and Queen Belle. Enjoy them in the knowledge that our kingdom is secure from the terrors of our past.

Auradon Prep Philosophy

Mission Statement
Helping the children of today
become the heroes and
heroines of tomorrow.

Heard Around Campus

"It's good to read other people's stories. It's better to write your own." —**Horace, librarian**

"Being incredible is harder than it looks, but I still suggest that everyone give it a try."
—**Chad, student**

"Inside every rapscallion lies the gleam of a heart of gold." —**Judy, guidance counselor**

"You can put a mermaid on dry land, but she has to learn to walk for herself." —**Abigail, biology teacher**

"I don't think it matters who your parents are, as long as they're beautiful and famous."
—**Audrey, student**

"If we don't try, we don't change. And if we don't change, we don't grow." —**Lonnie, student**

"Life's like Tourney. Sometimes it gets rough, but that's when you find your own fire." —**Coach Jenkins**

"Learning is a process of discovery, where the ultimate mystery is yourself."
—**Margaret, philosophy teacher**

"Bark, woof, bark!" Translation: "Go, Knights, Go!"
—**Dude the Dog**

Royal Roll Call

The living history of Auradon walks down our halls every day—Auradon Prep is filled with the heirs of illustrious kings, queens, fairies, dwarves, and wizards Take a peek at these family trees to see who's who.

Queen Belle — King Beast

Ben

Fairy Godmother

Jane

Fa Mulan — Li Shang

Lonnie

Dopey

Doug

Mal and the Gang,
orry we couldn't include
ou guys here. It was considered a little too
sky, since technically you guys aren't from
uradon. Maybe one day, I hope! —Ben

Queen
Aurora

King
Phillip

Because we're fearsome
villains, more like!
—Mal

Audrey

Queen
Cinderella

Prince
Charming

Chad

Slogans

Sleeping Beauty

"If you dream a thing more than once, it's sure to come true."

Belle

"Beauty is found within."

Mulan

"Follow your heart, and your mirror will show a true reflection."

Cinderella

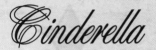

"A dream is a wish
your heart makes."

Fairy Godmother

"Faith creates miracles."

Dopey

"The best song is the
one anyone can sing."

Campus Points of Interest

Avenue of Heroes

On this very path, the founders of Auradon paraded to celebrate the creation of their new country. Today, it's the route every student takes to enter the school. Walk it enough and we're sure you'll find inspiration to become a hero, too.

King Beast's Statue

This unique work of enchanted art transforms from fearsome animal to noble human—King Beast's message that anyone can grow and change. NOTE: Students are asked not to scare others by standing behind the statue and making growling sounds.

Archimedes Library

A quiet place to study (no cursing allowed!) with a massive collection that features ancient texts like *Besting Vile Fairies* and *On Being a Proper Princess,* as well as today's bestsellers, including *A Buyer's Guide to Magical Swords* and *Love Without a Potion: Does It Exist?*

Scientific Labs

Our state-of-the-art research facility is dedicated to the great wizard whose slogan was, "Brain Over Brawn." Here we look into life's deepest mysteries, making discoveries that put the impossible within our grasp.

Tourney Field

Practice like a professional in our regulation arena! One-hundred-percent native Auradon grass provides perfect traction for sprinting down the field. Our reapers are the latest Titan 3000s, firing 100 rounds per minute. Strap on those cleats!

Cathedral

The birthplace of our fair country, this is where all the lands were unified in the very first coronation. Adorned with ornate stained glass windows depicting our history, the cathedral has an interior so massive it could host a dragon...in theory, anyway.

Dormitory Facilities

*A*uradon Prep's dorms make you feel like you're living in a palace—literally! Converted from the royal suites, they feature single and shared accommodations fit for princes, princesses, and all their friends.

Rooms are appointed with rugs and draperies, and the latest in home theater equipment. Computers have the fastest Internet connections in Auradon, making them excellent for playing online games. Just make sure you finish your homework first!

Tourney

Originally a training exercise and the Sport of Kings, Tourney was developed in the rebellion against Maleficent and her alliance of villains. Each side attempts to avoid a fearsome pair of cannons (the Reapers) as they make their way up the field (the Kill Zone) past the other team's defense to put the pontage into the net.

Message from MVP Chad

As Tourney's strongest player, I can tell you it's a man's game. Think you're up for it? You're welcome to try out. Even if you don't make the team, I'd be more than happy to give you some pointers. Work hard and you could be a Fighting Knight one day. (Maybe.)

Coach Jenkins' Corner

Alright, Princes—you're going to need courage, athletic skill, and even acrobatics if you want to win at Tourney. The good news? It's a team sport, so you don't have to be good at everything. Just focus on your own talent and you'll find your place. Study these famous strategies to see where you might fit in.

Excalibur: Team forms a sweeping line across the field like a giant blade, slicing through the defense.

Magic Carpet Ride: Players build a human platform and carry the captain to the enemy net.

Shield of Virtue: A defensive play in which the team forms a solid, impenetrable wall while singing the school song.

Infinity and Beyond: An advanced formation where players appear to fly across the field. (Actually, they are just falling with style.)

Cheer

Winner of the New Cheer Competition
By Audrey (Head Cheerleader)

Fighting Knights,
We're alright,
(Wait, are you serious?)
We're the B-E-S-T
Gonna crush ya, certainly!

Message from Audrey, Head Cheerleader

Hi! We already have the strongest squad on the continent, but don't let that discourage you from trying out! Ask yourself: Do I have a positive outlook, natural athletic ability, an innate sense of timing, and a perfect voice? And do people say you have a certain special something they can't put into words? If you answered an enthusiastic "Yes" to EVERY single one of these questions, you might just have what it takes to be on the squad.

Band

Message from Doug, Bandleader

Being in the band is about more than just playing an instrument— it's about creating big, beautiful pieces of music that make Auradon Prep. We have the largest and the best crew around, partly because we will include anyone who's interested. So if you can snap your fingers, tap your foot, or even hum tunelessly and you want to join up, come on down!

School Song Chorus

Auradon Prep
Fought the dragons of old.
Heroes we are,
Great blue and gold.

KNIGHTS

Annual Events

A roster of activities to look forward to this coming year

This should be called "Imprisoning all the cool people on the Isle of the Lost Day!" —Mal

		Unification Day Holiday
School Closed for Fairy Convention		
	Annual Singing Competition	**King Beast Honorary Holiday**
Science Fair		

This year, I swear my volcano will erupt! —Doug

Finally! My chance to sing "Let It Go" outside the shower! —Lonnie

Any roles for the most super-awesome leading lady?
I'll be in my dressing room. —Audrey

Auditions for School Play	No video game competition? There's room in the schedule right here. Come on, people! —Carlos		
Spirit Day		Family Day	
Heroes and Heroines Festival	When your mom's the principal, every day is Family Day... —Jane	Annual Knights Ball	
n. I'm all over —Jay	Archery Finals	Tourney Final	A perfect chance to test out some new...outfits!! —Evie
Hip Hop Dance Contest	Party at my place after they announce me MVP. No room for islanders— sorry! –Chad	Coronation	

So soon! Gulp! —Ben

Class Schedule

Block A: Chemistry
Block B: Safety Rules for the Internet
Block C: Grammar
Block D: History of Auradon

Block E: Enchanted Forestry
Block F: History of Woodsmen and Pirates
Block G: Mathematics
Block H: Remedial Goodness 101

Monday	Tuesday	Wednesday	Thursday	Friday
Homeroom 8:00 - 9:00	Block E 8:00 - 9:00	Block B 8:00 - 9:00	Free Block 8:00 - 9:00	Block D 8:00 - 9:00
Block A 9:00 - 10:00	Block F 9:00 - 10:00	Block C 9:00 - 10:00	Block G 9:00 - 10:00	Free Block 9:00 - 10:00
Block B 10:00 - 11:00	Block G 10:00 - 11:00	Free Block 10:00 - 11:00	Block H 10:00 - 11:00	Block E 10:00 - 11:00
Free Block 11:00 - 12:00	Block H 11:00 - 12:00	Block D 11:00 - 12:00	Block A 11:00 - 12:00	Block F 11:00 - 12:00
Lunch	Lunch	Lunch	Lunch	Lunch
Block C 1:00 - 2:00	Free Block 1:00 - 2:00	Block E 1:00 - 2:00	Block B 1:00 - 2:00	Block G 1:00 - 2:00
Block D 2:00 - 3:00	Block A 2:00 - 3:00	Block F 2:00 - 3:00	Block C 2:00 - 3:00	Block H 2:00 - 3:00

Bell Schedule

8:00 - 9:00 • 1st Period
9:00 - 10:00 • 2nd Period
10:00 - 11:00 • 3rd Period
11:00 - 12:00 • 4th Period
12:00 - 1:00 • Lunch
1:00 - 2:00 • 5th Period
2:00 - 3:00 • 6th Period

Sample Class Schedule

Text on chalkboard:
~WELCOME to REMEDIAL GOODNESS!~

#1- IF SOMEONE [hands] YOU A CRYING
BABY, DO [YOU:]
A) CURSE IT?
B) LOCK IT IN A TOWER?
[GIV]E IT A BOTTLE?
[TAK]E OUT IT'S HEART?

#2-YOU F[IND] [A BABY. DO] YOU:
[HIDE] IN THE KING'S WING?
[COOK] ON AN APPLE?
[TUR]N IT OVER TO THE PROPER
AUTHORITIES?

★ MOUTHS ARE FOR
SMILING, NOT FOR
BITING.

★ SHARING IS
CARING.

Remedial Goodness 101

This special course is designed to guide certain new students who might not have benefited from a strong moral upbringing. With a unique celebrity teacher, the Fairy Godmother, this promises to be a transformative educational experience. Learn:

- A bouquet is a much better present than cursing someone to eternal sleep.

- Hugs aren't meant for stabbing someone in the back.

- Doing evil weakens the immune system and may cause intestinal gas.

Bad Fairies

$\mathfrak{T}$elling a good fairy from an evil one can be more difficult than one might expect. But it will be easy once you've mastered this course! Curriculum includes:

- Understanding Bad Fairies—Empathize with these misunderstood creatures.

- Bad Fairy Encounters—How to show respect, especially if they're insecure about their tiny stature.

- If Things Get Nasty—Protecting yourself from an angry sprite using household objects.

Enchanted Forestry

$\mathfrak{L}$earn the names of all the ancient trees, their powers, and the complex pronunciation of their language. (HINT: It helps to place a piece of bark in your mouth.) Additional content includes:

- Root Handshakes—Proper grip can make th difference between an effective greeting and an unforgettable insult.

- Magical Toadstools—Some give you special powers, others put you to sleep for a hundre years...or longer.

- Grow Your Own Groot—From seed, in class!

History of Auradon

Which came first, the Rebellion or Maleficent's takeover? Who were the first King and Queen of Auradon, and who will be the next? What's our national dish, and who first cooked it? Discover the answers to these important questions in a course that's vital for every Auradon citizen.

Chemistry

Since the fading of magic, scientific discoveries have developed at a lightning pace. This course takes a deep dive into the structure of matter to see the incredible ways in which it behaves. You'll never look at the world around you—or yourself—in the same way again.

Dragon Anatomy

Discover the complex world of a dragon's insides, including its fire pouches and other vulnerable organs. Your mind will boggle at little-known facts, such as how to locate a dragon's wishbone, or how many people it takes to snap one (HINT: more than ten). Also learn basic care instructions for helping sick dragons beat a nasty cold. Trust us—this could save your life.

The Annual Auradon Wall

principal dear
have no fear
keep on smiling
ear to ear

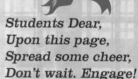

Students Dear,
Upon this page,
Spread some cheer,
Don't wait. Engage!

No thought or comment
Too sweet or bold.
Just open your heart,
Let the words unfold.

—*Fairy Godmother*

SOUNDS BORING!

What am I doing here?

Chad ~~is the worst~~ RULES!

Good/Evil???

47

Dear Coach,

I was wearing a mouth guard! —Jay

As a parent, I'm concerned about the barbarian nature of the new Tourney players—especially the one I think is named Jay (I found it difficult to understand (the grunts) these new players use to communicate).

Sounds like someone needs a lot of attention. —Mal

Word is getting around that "Jay" is taller and stronger than Ben. This is completely ridiculous. Also that he has the intensity of a born champion. Also a lie. It's true that Bennyboo sometimes seems a (little glazed over) but maybe that's just around his girlfriend, Audrey. She's wonderful!

Totes Malotes! —Evie

Could Bennyboo be (losing interest) in her?! He hasn't asked her out on a (picnic at the lake) Maybe he's intimidated. Who can blame him? As soon as he's crowned, he'll start seeing things on her level.

Was he ever interested? Seems like an arranged marriage to me. —Mal

I'm not a student, just a parental parent. Concerned about the Tourney team. Go, Fighting Knights!

Yours truly,
Mrs. P. Arent

Picnic shmicnic! But...I've only seen a lake on TV and the signal was pretty fuzzy. —Mal

48

Campus Morals and Ethics Committee
—Public Safety Announcement—

We would like to bring to your attention some truly shocking behavior witnessed in Chemistry class, perpetrated by one of the new students from the Isle of the Lost—Evie. It amounts to nothing less than the most horrible cheating!

The crime:
Use of a magic mirror to obtain the molecular weight of silver—as if she would even know what silver is!

We hoped for swift justice, but the sad truth is that Mr. Delay was far too lenient. He only threatened Evie with expulsion. Partially to blame is supporter/admirer/accomplice Doug, who—let's be honest—does not come from the smartest family.

It is our recommendation that Evie be considered guilty until proven innocent. Really, is there any point in holding a trial at all? Let's save school resources and simply send her back to her island. While we're at it, let's do the same with her boyfriend-stealing roommate, Mal.

Thank you for your time.
—CMEC

EXAMINATION
BOOKLET

Date of Examination

Student Name / ID#

Teacher Name

Subject

Dear Evie,

There was a time when you felt that you needed the mirror to succeed—kind of like having the deepest, darkest, magical training wheels. It's time to take those wheels off, girl. Seriously! You're smart enough to ride that bike all by yourself.

Go get 'em!

Love,
E.

Wow. I thought I'd be worried that you were writing letters to yourself—but I'm impressed with your positive coaching. Go, Evie! —Mal

Atomic Theory Unit Test

Section A: Multiple Choice

1. Which element contains a full 2p orbital in its valence shell?
   a) Ar   b) K   c) Mg   d) Ne   e) Sr

2. Which group of the periodic table does francium belong to?
   a) s block   b) p block   c) d block   d) f block   e) n block

3. What is the total number of electrons in the 3s orbital of a magnesium ion?
   a) 0   b) 1   c) 2   d) 3   e) 4

4. Identify the element given by the condensed electron configuration $[Ar]4s^23d^{10}4p^5$?
   a) Cl   b) Zn   c) Br   d) Cd   e) Kr

5. How many resonance structures would the compound O_3(ozone) have?
   a) 1   b) 2   c) 3   d) 4   e) 5

6. What is electron affinity?
   a) the energy that is required to completely remove one electron from a ground state gaseous atom
   b) the change in energy that occurs when an electron is added to a gaseous atom
   c) the size of the atomic sub-orbitals that electrons are found in
   d) the electromagnetic wavelength associated with an electron (e.g., visible, UV, X-ray)
   e) the energy required to form a new compound using valence electrons

7. The region of space in which there is a high probability of finding an electron is the definition of a(n)
   a) orbital   b) photon
   c) absorption spectrum   d) dipole
   e) quantum

8. What is the corresponding number of neutrons, protons, and electrons for the isotope iodine-131?
   a) 53N, 53P+, 53e-   b) 53N, 127P+, 53e-   c) 131N, 127P+, 53e-
   d) 78N, 53P+, 53e-   e) 74N, 53P+, 53e-

9. Place the following atoms in order of increasing atomic radius: Cl, F, Na, Li
   a) Li<F<Na<Cl   b) Na<Li<Cl<F   c) F<Cl<Li<Na   d) F<Cl<Na<Li

10. Electronegativity is best described as:
    a) the ease with which an atom is willing to accept an electron
    b) the ability of an electron to attract an electron toward itself within a covalent bond
    c) the energy required to remove the most weakly held electron from the valence shell
    d) the average distance from the nucleus to the valence shell

Auradon Prep

Hair-Raising Conspiracy

By Audrey

What some are calling "fashion forward" is an offense to our deepest values—an attack on our school, our country, our world!

Don't risk your reputatio by participating in these so-called acts of style. You' be conspiring with demons

Can you imagine Cinderella with asymmetri bangs? Or Snow White with a purple streak in her hair?! There is no use tryin to improve on perfection. What would our world be like if everyone expressed

While it may seem that Auradon Prep is going through a positive transformation, becoming more "groovy" and "cool," we are flying headlong into a cultural apocalypse.

emselves through
ow they look?
Mayhem!
It's true the
stigators may
ave grown up in a
ery exciting, edge-
-your-seat place
here anything goes.
ometimes that might
roduce a new look.
And sometimes
hen that look
atches your eye,
fills you with an
lectric thrill, a feeling
f freedom that you
an do anything.

But let me be
clear: That moment
passes quickly, as it
should. After all,
this is Auradon.

Ladies, we must
be strong! We must
contain ourselves.
We must look to
tradition. Hair may
seem like just a detail,
but it's way more. It's
a symbol. A symbol
that's under attack!
It's time we returned
this fiend to her place
of origin. Who's
with me?

Before

After

Hey, Jane—I think you're perfect already.
We all are, in our own way. It's just hard
to see sometimes. I know this sounds cheesy.
But I really mean it. Big hug! —Lonnie

Bet you need a microscope to see the difference.
Jane, I feel you, girl! It's tough around here. —M

Look, my dad has only three castles. And we can't use one because the carpets stink.
So will you please stop complaining? –Chad

have only one carpet—and it was born stinky. Love to ay at that vacant castle, Chad. Who wants to come? ane? We'll party like it's the Isle of the Lost! —Jay

I'm in! Can I bring Dude? Promise to shampoo him first! —Carlos

No way! My castle is not a rental! –Chad

ur parents really should look into that. xcellent passive income.—Doug

I don't think he needs the money. —Jay

Uh, guys...back to Jane? Girl, you're totally right. Talk about unrealistic expectations around here! Anytime you want to vent, knock on our dorm room. –Evie

Auradon

Auradon Prep

Chad Is Still the Best!

A Royal Reminder

By Anonymous

Imagine a world where everyone was royalty: a king or queen, prince or princess. It would be terrible! Nobody would know where they stood, who to look to for guidance. Everyone would be equal! Can you imagine anything more boring?

(continued from previous page)

Chad Is Still the Best

People might think you're cooler, some say better, Tourney players (which is totally insane). You'll soon discover you need to open your minds and accept your place in the system. So when I come to you for help with my homework, it's your opportunity to fit in, to contribute. Just like I do by being a leader. Hey, don't blame me for being right or charming. It runs in the family!

Fashion Flash! By Lonnie

There's a hot new fashion consultant in Auradon, and she's one of our very own students!

Some people are saying that because of where she comes from, Miss Evil Queen Jr. (Evie to her friends) has less to offer than those of us who were born here. But can you really say that after looking at some of her outfits?

It's true these looks might seem unusual. But I think they're fresh. Creativity is often surprising—that's what makes it creative! I'm proud to be at a school that has such talented students, even if their parents once tried to enslave us all. It's not like Evie wants to do that!

Isn't Auradon Prep about finding your own inner excellence? Then looking at Evie's ensembles should fill you with school spirit. Sure makes me feel that way.

Campus Cupid

The school can barely concentrate on its studies, with everyone trying to catch the latest on the biggest story of the year: Prince Ben is dating newcomer Mal, from the Isle of the Lost.

"She's the most amazing girl I've ever met," said the prince dreamily. "Did I mention that we're in love?"

Mal has been more difficult to pin down on the subject. We tried to interview her outside of Remedial Goodness 101, but she claimed she had a toothache. Later we knock on her dorm room door, but her roommate told us she was in the shower. We finally cornered her in the cafeteria.

"Yeah, Ben's alright," she said while sketching. "Not too terrible, I guess."

At the sound of his name,

> Darling Mal,
>
> This prince's best gal,
> My heart's on a platter,
> And nothing else matters
> But yoooouuuu!
>
> P.S. I love you!

Ben leaped from table to table (sending french fries flying) and began belting out yet another love ballad. Mal turned green and, declaring food poisoning, immediately ran from the dining hall.

Most worried about Ben's state of mind is ex-girlfriend Audrey.

"He must have hit his head or something," she said, adding, "I hope her wild island ways don't break Bennyboo's tender heart because I don't know what I'd do...to her. Cross out that last part?"

True love—or romantic disaster in the making? Only time will tell!

What do they think this is anyway, a movie? —Carlos

My mom always hogs the popcorn! —Mal
Who wants it anyway? She adds garlic powder! —Jay
Don't you think that looks like scheming? -Evie

Uh...no—just their resting evil faces. —Mal

Royal Proclamation

To: Staff, Students, and Parents of Auradon Prep
Subject: Videoconference with Isle of the Lost

We're gonna be on TV? Sweet! —Carlos

As some of you are aware, the upcoming Family Day allows students and parents an opportunity to visit with each other. This is an important date on our school calendar, which is why we're making an extra effort for our guest students from the Isle of the Lost to participate. Of course, security concerns render it impossible for their parents physically to enter the school (or the country). As an alternative, we will set up a videoconference that allows them to see and hear each other on television screens.

Yeah, but so is your mom. —Mal   *Forget it! I don't wanna be on TV. —Carlos*

For those not familiar with the technology, let me explain. Using satellites, a video of Mal and her friends will be relayed to the Isle of the Lost, where their parents will be watching. At the same time, their parents' video will be relayed to the school conference room. Rest assured: Our equipment will be scanned for any possible magical tampering. Only the images of the villains will reach the school—nothing more.

Sounds like a good steal. Where can we get one? —Jay

Thank you all in advance for your cooperation and ongoing commitment to cultural openness.

I think they're somewhere up in space. —Carlos

—King Beast

What's space? —Jay

Upcoming Coronation Details

**—On the Occasion of the Coronation
of His Majesty King Benjamin—**

By Command of King Beast and Queen Belle

All are invited to the Cathedral
on the fifth day of October
at three o'clock

Supper and Celebratory Dance to follow

Additional Instructions
Dress Code: Royal Fabulous*
Seating: See diagram
Note: Please inform us of any
food allergies in advance.

*Ceremonial swords not recommended.

*Actually, I'll be able to take in eve
more of the action. —Audrey*

You bet you're gonna have a great view of the action! —M

Cathedral Floor Plan

Well lookie here. It'll be front and
center now for little old me. —Mal

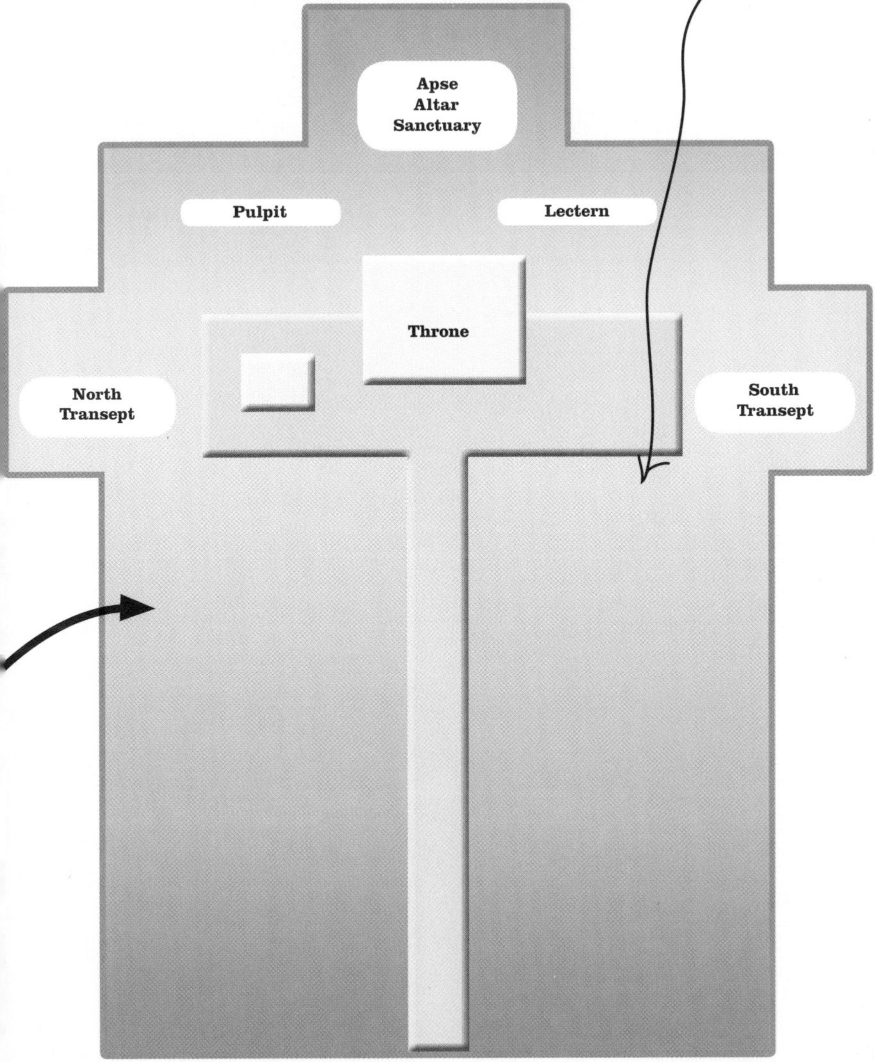

Apse
Altar
Sanctuary

Pulpit   Lectern

Throne

North   South
Transept   Transept

65

RADON
RADON
RADON
RADON
RADON
RADON

Campus Snapshots

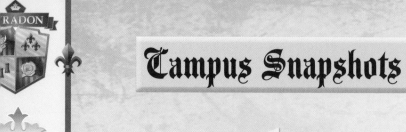

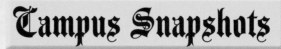

68

Family Day

Coronation
Program

Stoked to see that wand!
3:30 sharp, right guys? —Mal

Yes, ma'am! -Evie

I'm there! —Jay

oh, so that's what "half-after" means. —Carlos

Don't worry about the time—
I'll give you a hand signal. —Mal

Hand signal for
what? —Audrey

To be...really impressed. —Mal

Coronation Red Carpet

Talk about a perfect color! Mal stunned everyone with this floor-length gown. The beaded lace bodice has a subtle dragon-tail motif (how edgy!) and a very regal fan collar. A queen in the making? Mal is quick to credit fashionista Evie: "She's a genius!" We might not agree with much from the Isle of the Lost, but for this statement it's a big "Yes!" all around.

Is there a king in the house? Judging by Ben's gentlemanly ways, the future of Auradon is in very good hands. If this getup is any measure, we predict everyone's style to skyrocket by royal decree. Sure, it looks like just your average, amazingly tailored coronation suit—but get closer to see the inspired detailing that sets it even further apart. This outfit, and our royal friend who wears it, are both for the ages.

Even if your mother is an evil queen, you're still royalty—especially when you look so fabulous. This fashion phenomenon of the evening wows with a multilayered hi-lo skirt in textured chiffon, topped off with a ruched bodice featuring a gold-embroidered yoke. Add gold leather heels and a cape for effect (cool idea!), and runway chic takes on fairytale villainy. We dig it!

Some boys clean up well, while others clean up spectacularly. That's certainly the case with Jay, who traded his paint-stained graffiti gear for this maroon leather jacket. He's so handsome, Prince Charming might get nervous. Another hit from Evie, no doubt!

Can you say Rich Cultural Heritage? We hope so—because Lonnie's inspired version of the classic kimono left us all dazzled. In an elegant peach satin, the modern dress complements her perfectly. Finished off with jade earrings and a cool geometric peach-colored bracelet, this outfit looks historic and right now.

In this dusty blue formal gown, Jane shows that she can turn cute into a chic fashion statement. The ruffles and signature bow details are girlish on the one hand and ladylike on the other. And the glittery headpiece: what a great highlight! With delicately jeweled heart earrings and glamorous gold heels, this girl is representing—100%.

Taking a page straight from the family album, Chad's coronation style is a clear echo of his father's charming elegance. This light blue suit, crafted to perfection with no expense spared, seems to have actual gold detailing. How amazing! Hope he's wearing long underwear in case someone decides to steal that jacket and pants. Seriously—he's every inch a prince, helping make this a truly royal occasion.

Audrey always sets the tone for classic formalwear, and tonight was no exception. This rose-pink sequined gown shows yet again that she is none other than Sleeping Beauty's daughter, a proud keeper of tradition. Hot tip: Next time, take a walk on the wild side and try something out of Evie's playbook. She spices up your style, but keeps you true to your roots. What do you say, Audrey?

Kingdom Campus Security

Official Records

Entry No.	Date	Time
012578	Oct 5	4:45 PM

Incidents/Events for Record: Disturbance at Coronation

On this day and time we received a call from Auradon Prep student, Audrey, reporting the appearance of known criminal Maleficent at the coronation of Prince Benjamin.

Accidental discharge of Fairy Godmother's wand while in the possession of fellow student Jane resulted in a temporary shutdown of the energy field surrounding the Isle of the Lost. It would seem Maleficent used this opportunity to escape.

Suspect's reported intention was to steal aforementioned wand and, joining its power with her own staff, take control of Auradon. This would, of course, have resulted in the termination of civil freedoms and likely dictatorship. Candy privileges also certainly revoked.

Kingdom Ta

Official Records

Maleficent faced surprise resistance from her daughter, Mal, also of Auradon Prep. Suspect responded by transforming into giant dragon (see case #7/1Z33B) in order to roast everyone to a crisp.

Suspect's attack was foiled by Mal—and friends Evie, Jay, and Carlos—with a counter-spell causing her to shrink to the size of the love in her heart. Suspect altered from giant fire-breathing dragon to small pet lizard.

Campus security transferred suspect lizard to appropriate authorities, along with a cage, leash, food, and heat lamp.

Fairy Tale Celebration

Audrey, you smell like flowers...which are my favorite. —Jay

No, they aren't! —Carlos

Shut up, Carlos! —Jay   Thanks, Jay! —Audrey

oking like a regular princess! -Evie

Don't tell anyone, but it felt pretty awesome! —Mal

You earned it :) -Evie

AW! So Romantic. —Lonnie

Fairy Tale Celebration

This is the move I normally use on the guys.
—Audrey

Do that too much, and you might need a shoulder massage! —Jay

That an offer? —Audrey

Where'd you learn to dance like that? –Evie

My dad—he can really move. —Doug

Dopey? But he stands on someone's shoulders, right? –Evie

How do you think he taught me? —Doug

I'm sorry I let your mom out—I almost messed up this amazing party! —Jane

Don't sweat it! We probably wouldn't have had such a great time. —Mal

End of Year Review

Auradon Crystal Ball

MOST LIKELY TO...

Go on a First Date: *Jane*

Succeed: *Audrey*

Travel the World: *Lonnie*

Become a Pr[ofessional] Tourney Play[er]: *Jay*

Adopt a Pet: *Carlos*

84

Decree a Regular Royal Dance Party:
Ben

Book First Gallery Show:
Mal

Be Crowned Fairest of Them All:
Evie

Study Harder Next Year:
Chad

Receive a New Outfit from Evie:
Doug

Fellow Classmates,

It's been a wild ride. I started the year thinking that having big ideas was all it took to change things for the better, but it's much more complicated than that. It also takes a sense of adventure and fearless courage, things I understand a little better since I met our new friends from the Isle of the Lost. I'd like to thank them—and everyone. I couldn't be more proud of us all. Knowing I have such amazing people around me, I feel ready to give being king a shot.

Wish me luck!

Your friend,
—Ben

Hey Ben,

Looks like I'm not as evil as I thought, huh? Thanks for believing in me—and for teaching me to look to my heart. I like what I see there more than I ever thought possible. I'm starting my story over, and I couldn't be happier.

Yours, Mal

P.S. You're gonna make a great king!

P.P.S. To whoever finds this handbook: It seemed too good a tale to keep to ourselves. Hope you enjoyed it! We've left a few pages blank—in case you want to start a story of your own. Anything goes...as long as it's from the heart.

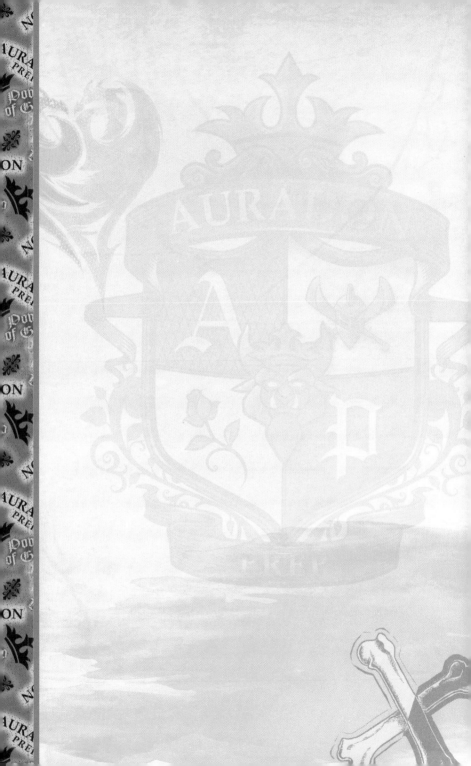

Studio Fun International
An imprint of Printers Row Publishing Group
A division of Readerlink Distribution Services, LLC
10350 Barnes Canyon Road, Suite 100, San Diego, CA 92121
www.studiofun.com